TENNESSEE WILLIAMS

THE TWO-CHARACTER PLAY

"A garden enclosed is my sister . . ."
Song of Solomon, 4:6

By TENNESSEE WILLIAMS

TENNESSEE WILLIAMS

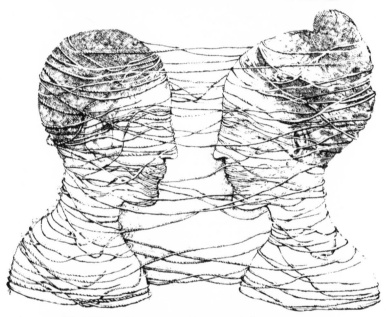

THE TWO-CHARACTER PLAY

A NEW DIRECTIONS BOOK

Two-Character Play was published in an earlier version as *Out Cry*

Manufactured in the United States of America

Published simultaneously in Canada by
Penguin Books Canada Limited

First published as New Directions Paperbook 483
(ISBN: 0–8112–0729–3) in 1979.

New Directions books are printed on acid-free paper

New Directions Books are published for James Laughlin
by New Directions Publishing Corporation,
80 Eighth Avenue, New York 10014

FIFTH PRINTING

The Two-Character Play opened at the Quaigh Theatre in New York on August 14, 1975, produced by William H. Lieberson (artistic director) and Martin Ewenstein (production coordinator), directed by Bill Lentsch, with Barbara Murphy as production stage manager and Debbie Tanklow as stage manager. The lighting and stage design were by Greg Husinko, the costumes by Isabelle Harris. The cast included Robert Stattel as Felice and Maryellen Flynn as Clare.

In the course of its evolution, several earlier versions of *The Two-Character Play* have been produced, the texts of which differ considerably from the one included in this volume. The first of them was offered at the Hampstead Theatre Club, London, on December 12, 1967, with Mary Ure and Peter Wyngarde, and James Rosse-Evans directing. The next, under the title *Out Cry,* was presented in Chicago on July 8, 1971, at the Ivanhoe Theatre. It was produced and directed by George Keathley, with Donald Madden and Eileen Herlie in the principal roles. Reworked, the play opened at the Lyceum Theatre in New York on March 1, 1973, produced by David Merrick Arts Foundation and Kennedy Center Productions, Inc., and directed by Peter Glenville. The lighting and stage design were by Jo Mielziner, the costumes by Sandy Cole, with Alan Hall as stage manager. The players were Michael York and Cara Duff-MacCormick.

SYNOPSIS OF SCENES

Before and after the performance: an evening in an unspecified locality.

During the performance: a nice afternoon in a deep Southern town called New Bethesda.

TENNESSEE WILLIAMS

THE TWO-CHARACTER PLAY

Before the performance.

The whole stage is used as the setting for the play, but at the front, in a widely angled V-shape, are two transparent, flat pieces of scenery which contain the incomplete interior of a living room in Southern summer. The stage-right flat contains a door, the other a large window looking out upon an untended patch of yard or garden dominated by a thick growth of tall sunflowers.

The furnishings of the interior are Victorian, including an old upright piano, and various tokens of the vocation of an astrologer, who apparently gave "readings" in this room. Perhaps the wallpaper is ornamented with signs of the Zodiac, the solar twelve-petaled lotus, and so on. (The designer should consult an astrologer about these tokens, which should give the interior an air of mystery. He might also find helpful a book called Esoteric Astrology).

About the stage enclosing this incomplete interior are scattered unassembled pieces of scenery for other plays than the play-within-a-play which will be "performed." Perhaps this exterior setting is the more important of the two. It must not only suggest the disordered images of a mind approaching collapse but also, correspondingly, the phantasmagoria of the nightmarish world that all of us live in at present, not just the subjective but the true world with all its dismaying shapes and shadows . . .

When the interior is lighted, it should seem to be filled with the benign light of a late summer afternoon: the stage surrounding should have a dusky violet light deepening almost to blackness at its upstage limits.

Of the unassembled set pieces which clutter this backstage area, the most prominent is a (papier-mâché) statue of a giant, pedestaled, which has a sinister look.

At curtain rise, FELICE, *the male star of an acting company on a tour which has been far more extensive than was expected, comes out of a shadowy area, hesitantly, as if fearful of the light. He has a quality of youth without being young. He is a playwright, as well as player, but you would be likely to take him for a poet with sensibilities perhaps a little deranged. His hair is almost shoulder length, he wears a great coat that hangs nearly to his ankles; it has a somewhat mangy fur collar. It is thrown over his shoulders. We see that he wears a bizarre shirt—figured with astrological signs—"period" trousers of soft-woven fabric in slightly varying shades of gray: the total effect is theatrical and a bit narcissan.*

He draws a piano stool into the light, sits down to make notes for a monologue on a scratch pad.

FELICE [*slowly, reflectively, writing*]: To play with fear is to play with fire. [*He looks up as if he were silently asking some question of enormous consequence.*] —No, worse, much worse, than playing with fire. Fire has limits. It comes to a river or sea and there it stops, it comes to stone or bare earth that it can't leap across and there is stopped, having nothing more to consume. But fear—

[*There is the sound of a heavy door slamming off stage.*]

Fox? Is that you, Fox?

[*The door slams again.*]

Impossible! [*He runs his hands through his long hair.*] Fear! The fierce little man with the drum inside the rib cage. Yes, compared to fear grown to panic which has no—what?— limits, at least none short of consciousness blowing out and not reviving again, compared to that, no other emotion a living, feeling creature is capable of having, not even love or hate, is comparable in—what?—force?—magnitude?

2

CLARE [*from off stage*]: Felice!

FELICE: —There is the love and the—substitutions, the surrogate attachments, doomed to brief duration, no matter how—necessary . . .—You can't, you must never catch hold of and cry out to a person, loved or needed as deeply as if loved —"Take care of me, I'm frightened, don't know the next step!" The one so loved and needed would hold you in contempt. In the heart of this person—him-her—is a little automatic sound apparatus, and it whispers, "Demand! Blackmail! Despicable! Reject it!"

CLARE [*in the wings*]: Felice!

FELICE: Clare! . . . What I have to do now is keep her from getting too panicky to give a good performance . . . but she's not easy to fool in spite of her—condition.

[CLARE *appears in the Gothic door to the backstage area. There is a ghostly spill of light in the doorway and she has an apparitional look about her. She has, like her brother, a quality of youth without being young, and also like* FELICE *an elegance, perhaps even arrogance, of bearing that seems related to a past theatre of actor-managers and imperious stars. But her condition when she appears is "stoned" and her grand theatre manner will alternate with something startlingly coarse, the change occurring as abruptly as if another personality seized hold of her at these moments. Both of these aspects, the grand and the vulgar, disappear entirely from the part of* CLARE *in "The Performance," when she will have a childlike simplicity, the pure and sad precociousness of a little girl.*

[A tiara, several stones missing, dangles from her fingers. She gives a slight startled laugh when she notices it, shrugs, and sets it crookedly on her somewhat disheveled and

3

streaked blonde head. She starts to move forward, then gasps and loudly draws back.]

Now what?

CLARE [*with an uncertain laugh*]: I thought I saw—

FELICE: Apparitions this evening?

CLARE: No, it was just my—shadow, it scared me but it was just my shadow, that's all. [*She advances unsteadily from the doorway.*] —A doctor once told me that you and I were the bravest people he knew. I said, "Why, that's absurd, my brother and I are terrified of our shadows." And he said, "Yes, I know that, and that's why I admire your courage so much . . ."

[FELICE *starts a taped recording of a guitar, then faces downstage.*]

FELICE: Fear is a monster vast as night—

CLARE: And shadow casting as the sun.

FELICE: It is quicksilver, quick as light—

CLARE: It slides beneath the down-pressed thumb.

FELICE: Last night we locked it from the house.

CLARE: But caught a glimpse of it today.

FELICE: In a corner, like a mouse.

CLARE: Gnawing all four walls away.

[FELICE *stops the tape.*]

CLARE [*straightening her tiara*]: Well, where are they, the ladies and gentlemen of the press, I'm ready for them if they are ready for me.

FELICE: Fortunately we—

4

CLARE: Hmm?

FELICE: —we don't have to face the press before this evening's performance.

CLARE: No press reception? Artists' Management guaranteed, Magnus personally promised, no opening without maximum press coverage on this fucking junket into the boondocks.—Jesus, you know I'm wonderful with the press... [*She laughs hoarsely.*]

FELICE: You really think so, do you, on all occasions?

CLARE: Know so.

FELICE: Even when you rage against fascism to a honking gaggle of—crypto-fascists? . . . With all sheets to the wind?

CLARE: Yes, sir, especially then.—You're terrible with the press, you go on and on about "total theatre" and, oh, do they turn off you and onto me . . . *Cockroach! Huge!* [*She stamps her foot.*] *Go!*—I read or heard somewhere that cockroaches are immune to radiation and so are destined to be the last organic survivors of the great "Amen"—after some centuries there's going to be cockroach actors and actresses and cockroach playwrights and—Artists' Management and—audiences . . . [*She gestures toward the audience.*]

FELICE: Have you got an "upper"?

CLARE: One for emergency, but—

FELICE: I think you'd better drop it.

CLARE: I never drop an upper before the interval. What I need now is just coffee. [*She is struggling against her confusion.*] —Tell Franz to get me a carton of steaming hot black coffee. I'm very annoyed with Franz. He didn't call me . . . [*She laughs a little.*] —Had you forbidden him to?

[*There is no response.*]

5

So I'm left to while the long night away in an unheated dressing room in a state theatre of a state unknown—*I have to be
told when a performance is canceled!*—or won't perform!
[*Her tiara slips off. She crouches unsteadily to retrieve it.*]

FELICE: The performance has not been canceled and *I*
called you, Clare.

CLARE: After I'd called you.

FELICE: I have some new business to give you, so come
here.

CLARE: I'll not move another step without some—Oh,
light, finally something almost related to *daylight*! But it's
not coming through a window, it's coming through a—

FELICE [*overlapping*]:—There's a small hole in the backstage wall. [*He crosses to look out at the audience.*] They're
coming in.

CLARE: Do they seem to be human?

FELICE: No.—Yes! It's nearly curtain time, Clare.

CLARE: Felice! Where is everybody?—I said, "Where *is*
everybody?"

FELICE: Everybody is somewhere, Clare.

CLARE: Get off your high horse, I've had it!—Will you
answer my question?

FELICE: No cancelation!

CLARE: No show!

FELICE: What then?—In your contrary opinion?

CLARE: *Restoration* of—*order*!

FELICE: What order?

CLARE: Rational, rational! [*Her tiara falls off again.*]

6

FELICE: Stop wearing out your voice before the—

CLARE: Felice, I hear gunfire!

FELICE: I *don't*!

CLARE [*sadly*]: We never hear the same thing at the same time any more, *caro* . . . [*She notices a throne-chair, canopied, with gilded wooden lions on its arms: on the canopy, heraldic devices in gold thread.*] Why, my God, old Aquitaine Eleanor's throne! I'm going to usurp it a moment— [*She mounts the two steps to the chair and sits down in a stately fashion, as if to hold court.*]

FELICE [*holding his head*]: I swear I wouldn't know my head was on me if it wasn't aching like hell.

CLARE: What are you mumbling?

FELICE: An attack of migraine.

CLARE: You'd better take your codeine.

FELICE: I've never found that narcotics improve a performance, if you'll forgive me for that heresy, Clare.

CLARE: —Is this tour nearly over?

FELICE: It could end tonight if we don't give a brilliant performance, in spite of—

CLARE: Then it's over, *caro,* all over . . . How long were we on the way here? All I remember is that it would be light and then it would be dark and then it would be light and then dark again, and mountains turned to prairies and back to mountains, and I tell you honestly I don't have any idea or suspicion of where we are now.

FELICE: After the performance, Clare, I'll answer any question you can think of, but I'm not going to hold up the curtain to answer a single one now!

7

CLARE [*rising*]: —Exhaustion has—symptoms . . .

FELICE: So do alcohol and other depressants less discretely mentioned.

CLARE: I've only had half a grain of—

FELICE: Washed down with liquor, the effect's *synergistic.* Dr. Forrester told you that you could have heart arrest—*on stage!*

CLARE: Not because of anything in a bottle or box but—

FELICE [*overlapping*]: What I know is I play with a freaked out, staggering—

CLARE [*overlapping*]: Well, play with yourself, you long-haired son of a mother!

FELICE [*overlapping*]: Your voice is thick, slurred, you've picked up—vulgarisms of—gutters!

CLARE [*overlapping*]: What you pick up is stopped at the desk of any decent hotel.

FELICE [*overlapping*]: *Stop it!* I can't take any more of your—

CLARE [*overlapping*]: *Truth!*

FELICE [*overlapping*]: *Sick, sick—aberrations!*

[*There is a pause.*]

CLARE [*like a child*]: When are we going home?

FELICE: —Clare, our home is a theatre anywhere that there is one.

CLARE: If this theatre is home, I'd burn it down over my head to be warm a few minutes . . . You know I'm so blind I can't go on without crawling unless you—

FELICE: Wait a minute, a moment, I'm still checking props
—bowl of soapwater but only one spool . . .

[CLARE *encounters the Gothic, wood figure of a Madonna.*]

CLARE: —You know, after last season's disaster, and the
one before last, we should have taken a long, meditative rest
on some Riviera instead of touring these primitive, God-
knows-where places.

FELICE: You couldn't stop any more than I could, Clare.

CLARE: If you'd stopped with me, I could have.

FELICE: With no place to return to, we have to go on, you
know.

CLARE: And on, till finally—here. I was so exhausted that
I blacked out in a broken-back chair.

FELICE: I'm glad you got some rest.

CLARE [*hoarsely*]: The mirrors were blind with dust—my
voice is going, my voice is practically gone!

FELICE: —Phone where? Piano top. No. Table.—Yes, you
never come on stage before an opening night performance
without giving me the comforting bit of news that your voice
is gone and . . . [*Imitating her voice:*] "I'll have to perform in
pantomime tonight."

CLARE: Strike a lucifer for me.

[*He strikes a match and she comes unsteadily into the interior set: he gives her a despairing look.*]

FELICE: —Why the tiara?

CLARE [*vaguely*]: It was just in my hand, so I put it on my
head.

[*He gives a little hopeless laugh.*]

9

I try like hell—how I try—to understand your confusions, so why don't you make some effort to understand mine a little?

FELICE: Your variety's too infinite for me, Clare.

CLARE: —You still can't forgive me for my Cleopatra notices. Ran into columns of extravagance and your Anthony's were condensed as canned milk.

FELICE: —Do you hate me, Clare?

CLARE: I think that's a question I should be putting to you. The night we opened in . . . [*She tries to remember the place, can't.*] —you turned on me like a spit-devil and shouted—Oh, I'd rather not quote you!

FELICE: Do. Please.

CLARE: —You called me a drunken slut and said "Fuck off!"

FELICE: —You can't believe I said that.

CLARE: Oh, let it go, it's gone . . . [*She starts toward the proscenium.*] Think I'll have a look at the enemy forces.

FELICE [*seizing her wrist*]: You will not, you must never look at an audience before a performance. It makes you play self-consciously, you don't get lost in the play.

CLARE: Never catch hold of my wrist like that, it leaves blue bruises! [*She has struck his hand away.*] Why are you so—wildly distracted, *cher*?

FELICE: I'm living on my nerves and they're—I'll probably dry up several times tonight but— [*He quickly exits to light the interior set.*]

CLARE [*looking about*]: Oh, God, this is the set for "The Two-Character Play," but where's the stairs and—?

10

FELICE [*returning*]: So far only parts of the set have arrived.

CLARE: What will I do when I'm supposed to go upstairs for parasol and gloves?

FELICE: Face upstage and I'll say you've gone upstairs. Your parasol and gloves are on top of the piano.

CLARE: Are you serious? About playing it this way?

FELICE: Desperately.

CLARE: Are you going to throw new speeches at me tonight?

FELICE: Tonight there'll have to be a lot of improvisation, but if we're both lost in the play, the bits of improvisation won't matter at all, in fact they may make the play better. [*He smiles wryly.*]

CLARE: I like to know what I'm playing and especially how a play ends.

FELICE: When the curtain is up and the lights are on, we'll fly like birds through the play, and if we dry up, we'll use it.

CLARE: Felice, do you have a fever?

[FELICE *has crossed to the proscenium.*]

There you go peeking out again, and you won't let me.

FELICE: I have to see if they're in or—

CLARE: We have no communication with the front of the house? [*She coughs and spits.*]

FELICE: None.

CLARE: You mean we're—?

FELICE: Isolated. Completely.

11

CLARE: —I need a month at a little—Bavarian—spa.

FELICE: You know, that "high" you're on is going to wear off in about half an hour and you'll have the energy of a piece of seaweed at low tide . . . Immediately after this tour I suggest that you enter a clinic for withdrawal from—

CLARE [*shouting*]: *After this tour is when? When will there be an end to it?*

FELICE: Soon.

CLARE: Make it sooner! Cancel the rest and let's—*rest!*

FELICE: Do you want to cross back over forty, fifty frontiers on wooden benches in third-class coaches?

CLARE: —You mean that—?

FELICE: I mean that's the style we'd make our triumphant return in if we turned back now without playing a week in the black since—

CLARE: —How big a hole are we in?

FELICE: Big enough to bury an elephant team.

CLARE: Why haven't you told me these things?

FELICE: It's impossible to have a realistic discussion with someone who's—[*He holds up three fingers.*] How many fingers am I holding up?

CLARE: You know I don't have my—my God, yes, I do! [*she fumblingly removes a pair of "granny" glasses from a pocket in her cloak-lining. She crosses directly to Felice, head tilted back to peer into his face.*] Oh, Felice, you look so terribly tired!

FELICE: Those glasses make you look—

CLARE: Ancient? Well—they don't subtract many years from you either.—Do you mind if I make one more comment on your appearance—if it's tactfully worded?

FELICE: I've had no time to make up.

CLARE: This comment's on your hair, why, it's almost as long as mine.

FELICE: You know I wear a wig for the role of Felice.

CLARE: The part of Felice is not the only part that you play.

FELICE: From now on, it might be.

CLARE: Wouldn't *that* please the Company! What would they be doing?

FELICE: I don't have any idea or a particle of interest.

CLARE: Oh! How regal!

[FELICE *pounds the stage floor three times with a staff.*]

Listen to that!

FELICE: I hear it.

CLARE: It sounds like a house full of furiuos, unfed apes.

FELICE: Maybe it is.

CLARE: Felice—where is everybody?

[*He pounds the stage floor again.*]

I asked you where is everybody and I *insist* on an answer.

FELICE: Oh, you *insist* on an answer! You're sure you want an answer?

CLARE: Yes, I do, right now!

FELICE: Perhaps you'll find this more illuminating than I did. [*He hands her a piece of paper.*]

CLARE: Oh. A cablegram?

FELICE: Yes!

CLARE: I can't make it out in this sepulchral—

FELICE: —Never mind, Clare, give it back.

CLARE: Not if it has to do with—strike a match!

[*He does. She reads aloud, slowly, in a shocked voice.*]

"Your sister and you are—*insane!*—Having received no pay since—"

[*The match burns out.*]

Strike another!

[*He does.*]

"We've borrowed and begged enough money to return to—"

FELICE: Signed: "The Company." Charming? [*He blows the match out.*]

CLARE: My God! Well, as they say— [*She turns to the piano and strikes a note.*]

FELICE: What do they say?

CLARE: That sort of wraps things up!

FELICE: The Company's left us, except for two stage hands who came in without a word and put up this piece of the set before they—

CLARE: Deserted us, too?

FELICE [*again at the proscenium, looking out*]: Now, then, they're finally seated!

14

CLARE [*retreating from the proscenium*]: —Felice, I am going to the hotel, that's where you'll find me when you've recovered your senses, I am going straight there and collapse because I would rather collapse in my hotel room than on a stage before people stranger than strangers.

FELICE: What hotel did you think you were going to, Clare?

CLARE: —Whichever—hotel we—stay at . . .

FELICE: Do you recall checking into a hotel, Clare?

CLARE: —When?

FELICE: Yes, when? After we got off the train, before we came to the theatre, is that when?

CLARE: Are you telling me that Fox hasn't made hotel reservations for us?

FELICE: Fox has done one thing. No, two: he demanded his salary—which I couldn't pay him—and after that, disappeared.

[*She gasps.* FELICE *holds out his hand toward her. Looking desolately into space, she places her hand in his.*]

Clare, I was holding out my hand for your coat.

CLARE: Do you think I'm about to remove my coat in this ice-plant?

FELICE: We're in our home, Clare, in the deep South and in summer.

CLARE [*hugging her coat about her*]: Let's—synchronize— thermometers and—geographies.

[*He suddenly tears the coat off her, and she cries out*]

FELICE [*pointing downstage at the supposed curtain*]: Hush.

15

CLARE: You're a monster!

FELICE: Yes, if you wish. Take your place.

[*She snatches up her coat, which he had flung onto the sofa.*]

CLARE: I'll wait in my dressing room till you've announced the performance is canceled. *Where are you—?*

[*He is striding toward the wings.*]

FELICE [*turning to hiss at her furiously*]: Will you take your place? I'm going to open the curtains!—Now, this instant!

CLARE: Are you serious?

FELICE: Desperately!

CLARE: Impossible!

FELICE: Necessary.

CLARE: Some necessary things are impossible.

FELICE: And some impossible things are necessary. We are performing tonight.

[*She stares at him a moment: then strikes a sharp note on the piano.*]

CLARE: I told you that I would not perform again in *The Two-Character Play* until you had cut it. Have you? Have you cut it?

FELICE [*evasively*]: Where my work is concerned—

CLARE: I said *have you cut it?*

FELICE: You're given cuts when I make them.

CLARE: I'm not going to be given cuts, I'm going to make them myself. Now can you hear this C-sharp on the piano?

16

[*She strikes a note on the piano.*] Whenever you hear this C-sharp struck on the piano it means a cut's coming at you, and don't try to duck it or I'll take a walk.

FELICE: This is—

CLARE: *Sacrilege?*

FELICE: —*Idiocy!*

CLARE: Total theatre is going to be total collaboration on this occasion, ducks.

FELICE: —Take your place.

CLARE: My place is here at the phone.

FELICE [*pointing to the window frame*]: Your place is—

CLARE: *Here* at the *phone!*

FELICE: You—*mother!*—May I have the tiara?

[*She smiles with fierce mockery: removes the tiara from her head and places it crookedly on his. He hurls it away.*]

You—castrating bitch, you—drunk—*slut!* Yes, I did call you that, I don't look at you on stage because I can't bear the sight of your—eyes, they're eyes of an—old demented— whore! Yes, a water-front whore! Lewd, degenerate, leering!

CLARE: I see!

FELICE: No, no, no, you don't see, you're *bl-i-i-nd!*

[*He stalks into the wings. She stands shocked motionless for a moment: then snatches up her cloak and throws it about her. She starts a few steps toward the opposite wings when the interior set is flooded with warm amber light and the curtains are heard jerking spasmodically open. She freezes. There are several guttural exclamations from the house: above them, a hoarse male laugh and the shrill*]

17

laugh of a woman. CLARE'S *eyes focus blazingly on the "house": She suddenly flings her cloak to the floor as if challenging the audience to combat.* FELICE *returns to the stage. He inclines his head toward* CLARE: *then toward the house.*]

The performance commences!

[*The performance. Clare is at the phone.*]

FELICE: Who are you calling, Clare?

[*She seems not to hear him.*]

Clare! Who are you calling?

CLARE: —Not a soul still existing in the world gone away . . .

FELICE: Then why did you pick up the phone?

CLARE: I just picked it up to see if it's still connected.

FELICE: The telephone company would send us a notice before they turned off the phone.

CLARE [*vaguely and sadly*]: Sometimes notices aren't— noticed.

FELICE: The house is—

CLARE: Still occupied but they might have the idea it wasn't, since it's not lighted at night and no one still comes and goes.

FELICE: We would have received a notice if one was sent.

CLARE: We can't count on that.

FELICE: We mustn't start counting things that can't be counted on, Clare.

CLARE: We must trust in things—

FELICE: Continuing as they've—

CLARE: Continued?

FELICE: Yes, as they've continued, for such a long time that they seem—

CLARE: Dependable to us.

FELICE: Permanently dependable, yes, but we were—

CLARE: Shocked when the—

FELICE: Lights refused to turn on, and it was lucky the moon was so nearly full that, with the window shades raised, it lighted the downstairs rooms.

CLARE: But we collided with things in the upstairs hall.

FELICE: Now we could find our way around in it blind.

CLARE: We can, we do. Without even touching the walls.

FELICE: It's a small house and we've lived in it always.

[CLARE *strikes C-sharp: he glares at her; she strikes it repeatedly. In a fierce whisper:*] *I will not cut into texture!*

CLARE: There's more about night. You tell me that I was indulging in a bit of somnambulism, last night?

FELICE: Clare, you had a sleepless night.

CLARE: And you did, too.

FELICE: In a small house when one of the occupants has a sleepless night, it keeps the other awake.

CLARE [*crying out*]: *Why do I have to sleep in that death chamber?*

FELICE [*controlled*]: We agreed that their room was just a room now. Everything about them's been removed.

19

CLARE: Except Father's voice in the walls and his eyes in the ceiling.—That night of the accident night I had to force my way past you to the room where—Mother opened the door . . .

FELICE [*cutting her off*]: Stop repeating, repeating!

CLARE: No sign of recognizing me at the door, no greeting, a look of surprise, very slight, till she opened her mouth on a soundless fountain of blood, and Father said, "Not yet, Clare," just as quietly, gently to me as *that,* before they went separate ways, she to the door of the bathroom where she fell and he to the window where he fired again looking out at—*out . . .*

[FELICE *strikes his fist on the piano keys.*]

And you tell me it isn't their room any more?

FELICE: I said: "LET IT REST!"

CLARE: Not in that room at night!

FELICE [*with forced quiet*]: You weren't in that room last night, you wandered about the house, upstairs and down, as if you were looking for something.

CLARE: Exploring the premises, yes . . .

FELICE: With a fine tooth comb as if you suspected there was a time bomb somewhere.

CLARE: I could almost hear it ticking.

FELICE: Well? Did you find it?

CLARE: No, but I did find something, this old memento, this token of—

FELICE [*starting the tape recorder*]: What?

CLARE [*lifting her hand*]: My ring with my birthstone, the opal.

20

FELICE: You haven't worn it for so long that I thought it was lost.

CLARE: Mother told me that opals were unlucky.

FELICE: Frigid women are given to little fears and superstitions, and—

CLARE: Opals do have a sinister reputation. And it was a gift from Father.

FELICE: That was enough to prejudice her against it.

CLARE: Sleepless people love rummaging. I look through pockets that I know are empty. I found this ring in the pocket of an old mildewed corduroy coat which I'd forgotten I'd ever owned and didn't care if the stone was unlucky or not.

FELICE: Nothing could be unlucky that looks so lovely . . .

[*He turns the ring on her finger—a sort of lovemaking. She strikes the piano key.*]

CLARE [*regaining her composure somewhat*]: Didn't you tell me you went out today?

FELICE: Yes, you saw me come in.

CLARE: I didn't see you go out.

FELICE: When you see somebody come in you know he's been out.

CLARE [*skeptically*] How far outside did you go? Past the sunflowers, or—?

FELICE: I went to the gate, and do you know what I noticed?

CLARE: Something that scared you back in?

FELICE: No, what I saw didn't scare me, but it, it—*startled* me, though. It was—

21

CLARE: What?

FELICE: Clare.

CLARE: What?

FELICE [*in a stage whisper*]: You know *The Two-Character Play.*

CLARE [*in a loud stage whisper*] The cablegram is still on the set.

FELICE: Clare, there wasn't, there isn't a cablegram in *The Two-Character Play.*

CLARE: Then take it off the sofa where I can see it. When you see a thing, you can't think it doesn't exist, unless you're hallucinating and you know that you are.

[*He picks up the cablegram, crumples it, and makes a gesture of throwing it out the window.*]

FELICE: There now, it never existed, it was just a moment of panic.

CLARE: What a convenient way to dispose of a panicky moment!

FELICE: Dismissed completely, like that! [*He snaps his fingers.*] And now I'll tell you what I saw in the yard when I went out.

CLARE: Yes, do that! Do, please.

FELICE: I saw a sunflower out there that's grown as tall as the house.

CLARE: Felice, you know that's not so!

FELICE: Go out and see for yourself.

[*She tries to laugh.*]

22

Or just look out the window, it's in the front yard, on this side.

CLARE: *Front* yard?

[*He nods but averts his face with a slight smile.*]

Now I know you're fooling.

FELICE: Oh, no, you don't or you'd go look out the window for yourself, it's shot up as quick as Jack's beanstalk and it's so gold, so brilliant that it—[*He sits on the sofa and seems to be musing aloud.*]—it seems to be shouting sensational things about us. [*He gives her a quick, sly look.*] Tourists will be attracted, botanists—you know botanists—will come to—marvel at this marvel, photograph it for the—the *National Geographic,* this marvel of nature, this two-headed sunflower taller than a two-story house which is still inhabited by a recluse brother and his sister.

CLARE: It would be a monster of nature, not marvel, if it existed at all, and I know that it doesn't.

[*She strikes a warning note on the piano. He snatches her hand off the keyboard and slams the piano lid shut; then sits on it, grinning at her mockingly.*]

FELICE: You know, I wonder if nature, that vast being and producer of beings, is satisfied with so many of its beings being so much like so many others of that kind of being or would actually be better pleased with more little—prodigies? Monsters? Freaks? Mute relations?—What's your opinion, Clare?

CLARE: No opinion, no comment, no recollection of lines!

FELICE: My opinion is that nature is tolerant of and sometimes favorable to these—differentiations if they're—usable? Constructive?—But if you're not, watch out you!

23

CLARE: You watch out.

[*She snatches up her cloak. He rises from the piano lid.*]

FELICE: —Why don't you go to the door? Don't you hear them knocking?

CLARE: Who?

FELICE: I can't see through the door.

CLARE: I don't hear any knocking. [*He drums the piano lid with his knuckles.*] —Oh, yes, now, I do, but—

FELICE: See who's there.

CLARE: I can't imagine.

FELICE: You don't have to imagine, you can go to the door and—

CLARE: *You* go.

[*There are audible whispers.*]

You're closer to it than I am, and—

[*He knocks the table harder.*]

—They're very—insistent, aren't they?

FELICE: It must be something important, go on, see what it is.

CLARE: I'm—not dressed for callers.

FELICE: You're prefectly dressed and look extremely well.

CLARE [*retreating further from the door*]: So do you aside from your hair.

FELICE: I don't have a tie on, and this old shirt of father's, I've sweated through it.

CLARE: That's, uh, excusable on a—hot afternoon. You, uh, let them in and say you'll call me down if it's *me* they—want to see *me*.

FELICE: Have you reached the point where you're scared to answer a door?

CLARE: Reached and—the knocking's stopped.—I think they've gone away, now.—No! Look! They're slipping a piece of paper under the door!

[*They stare fearfully at the supposed piece of paper on the doorsill.*]

FELICE: —They've left.

CLARE: Yes! Pick up the—

[*He crosses to the door, and makes the gesture of picking up a card, then frowns at it.*]

—What is—?

FELICE: A card from something called "Citizens' Relief."

CLARE: Then people know we're still here?

FELICE: Naturally, yes, where would we be but still here? —"Citizens' Relief"—I've never heard of it. Have you?

CLARE: No, and I think it's wise to be cautious about things you've—

FELICE: Never heard of.

CLARE: It might be a trick of some kind.

FELICE: It might be an excuse to intrude on our—

CLARE: Privacy, yes. Shall we destroy the card or keep it in case of a desperate situation?

FELICE: The case of a desperate situation isn't a thing we have to wait for, is it?

CLARE: Oh, but all the questions we'd have to—

FELICE: —Answer . . .

CLARE: Yes, there'd be interviews and questionnaires to fill out and—

FELICE: Organizations are such—

CLARE: *Cold!*

FELICE: Yes, impersonal things.

CLARE: I'll put the card under grandmother's wedding picture, just in case a desperate situation—

FELICE: Increases in desperation . . .

CLARE: Anyway, here it is, at least we—know where it is— What's next on the agenda? Do I pick up the phone? No, no, I pick up this sea shell, hold it to my ear, and remember the time that Father took us to the sea coast.

FELICE: It was the Gulf coast. [*He starts the tape again.*]

CLARE: The Gulf connects with a sea, it has gulls, tides, dunes—

FELICE: Much against Mother's objections, he took us there one summer when we were children, before we had started to school—

CLARE: Mother refused to stay at The Lorelei on the beach, we had to stay at the Hotel Commerce, back of the business district, and walk to the Municipal in bathing suits that hung down to our knees, and Mother never stopped nagging: "I checked with the cashier at the hotel. We can only afford a day more."

FELICE: Father would grin up lazily from the sand but finally shout out furiously at her: "Go back to the Hotel Commerce, continue your mathematical talk with the cashier, subtract, divide if you can, but don't multiply, and don't stay here in the sun, it disagrees with you!"

CLARE: And he'd snatch us up and away we would race, away . . .

FELICE: —Away from the Municipal, past the lighthouse tower and into the sand dunes where he tore off his suit and looked so much more elegant without it that we tore off ours, and he carried me into the water on his smooth gold shoulders and I learned to swim as if I'd always known how to . . .

CLARE [*pointing out toward the audience*]: Felice—someone's talking out there with his back to the stage as if he were giving a lecture.

FELICE: That's the interpreter.

CLARE: Oh, my God, he's telling them what we're saying!?

FELICE: Naturally, yes, and explaining our method. That's what he's here for.

CLARE [*half sobbing*]: I don't know what to do next—I . . .

FELICE: —I know what to do.

CLARE: Oh, do you? What is it? To sit there staring all day at a threadbare rose in a carpet until it withers?

FELICE: Oh, and what do you do? What splendid activity are you engaged in, besides destroying the play?

CLARE: None, none, nothing, unless it's something to pace about the house in a maze of amazement all day and sometimes in the night, too. Oh, I know why!

FELICE: Why?

CLARE: I want to go out! *Out, out, human outcry, I want to go out!*

FELICE: You want to go out calling?

CLARE: Yes, out calling!

FELICE: Go out!

CLARE: *Alone?*—Not *alone!*

FELICE: Ladies go calling alone on such nice afternoons.

CLARE: You come out calling with me.

FELICE: I can't, I have to stay here.

CLARE: For what?

FELICE: —To guard the house against—

CLARE: What?

FELICE: *Curious—trespassers!* Somebody has to stay on the premises and it has to be me, but you go out calling, Clare. You must have known when you got up this morning that the day would be different for you, not a stay-at-home day, of which there've been so many, but a day for going out calling, smiling, talking. You've washed your hair, it's yellow as corn silk, you've pinned it up nicely, you have on your blue-and-white print that you washed to go out in today and you have the face of an angel, Claire, you match the fair weather, so carry out your impulse, go out calling. You know what you could do? Everywhere you went calling you could say, "Oh, do you know how idiotic I am? I went out without cigarettes!" And they'd offer you one at each place and you could slip them into your purse, save them till you got home, and we could smoke them here, Clare. So! Go! [*He opens the door for her.*]

CLARE: Why have you opened the door?

FELICE: For you to go out calling.

CLARE: Oh, how thoughtful yes, that's very gentleman of you to open the door for me to go outside without parasol or gloves, but not very imaginative of you to imagine that I'd go out alone.

[*They stand a moment staring at each other near the open door: her hands and lips tremble; the slight smile, mocking and tender, twists his mouth.*]

—Suppose I came home alone, and in front of the house there was a collection of people around an ambulance or police car or both? We've had that happen before . . . No. I won't go out alone. [*She slams the door shut.*] My legs wouldn't hold me up, and as for smiling and talking, I'd have on my face the grimace of a doll and my hair would stick to the sweat of my forehead. Oh, I'd hardly sit down for this friendly call on—*what* friends?—before I—staggered back up, that is, if, if—the colored girl had been allowed to admit me.

FELICE: It was your idea. *You* shouted: "Out!" Not me.

CLARE: I'd never dream of going out without you in your —disturbed—*condition.*

FELICE: And *you* in *yours.*

CLARE: Me, calling, a fire engine shrieks, a revolver— bang!—discharges! Would I sit there continuing with the smile and the talk? [*She is sobbing a little: her trembling hand stretches toward him.*] No, I'd spring up, run, run, and my heart would stop on the street!

FELICE [*his smile fading out*]: I never believed you'd go out calling.

CLARE: Right you were about that if you thought alone— but calling? Yes, I'll do that! Phone calling is calling! [*She rushes to the telephone and snatches up the receiver.*]

FELICE: Calling, who are you—? *Careful!*

CLARE [*into phone*]: Operator, the Reverend Mr. Wiley! Urgent, very, please hurry!

[*Felice tries to wrest the phone from her grasp: for a moment they struggle for it.*]

FELICE: Clare!

CLARE: Reverend Wiley, this is Clare Devoto, yes, you remember, the daughter of—

FELICE: What are you? Out of your—?

CLARE: You'll have to let me go on or he'll think I'm— [*into the phone again*:] Excuse me, Riverend Wiley, there was—an interruption. My brother and I still live in our parents' home after, after the—terrible accident in the house which was reported so maliciously falsely in *The Press-Scimitar.* Father did *not* kill Mother and himself but—

FELICE: Tell him *we* shot them why don't you?

CLARE: The house was broken into by some—

FELICE: Favorite of nature?

CLARE: Housebreaker who murdered our parents, but I think *we* are suspected! My brother Felice and I are surrounded by so much suspicion and malice that we almost never, we hardly ever, dare to go out of the house. Oh, I can't tell you how horrifying it's been, why, the neighbor's child has a slingshot and bombards the house with rocks, we heard his *parents* give the slingshot to him and *tell* him to— —*Ha! Another rock struck just now!*—It goes on all through the daytime, and in the nighttime people stop and linger on the sidewalk to whisper charges of—anomalous letters of obscenities are sent us, and in *The Press-Scimitar*—sly allusions to us as the·deranged children of a father who was a false mystic and, Reverend Wiley, our father was a man who had true psychic, mystical powers, granted only to an Aries whose element is cardinal fire. [*She is sobbing now.*]—Why? We're gentle people, never offending a soul, trying to still live only, but—

[FELICE *wrests the phone from her hands.*]

FELICE: Mr. Wiley, my sister has a fever.

CLARE: No, I—!

FELICE: She's not herself today, forget what, excuse and— [*He hangs up, wipes the sweat off his forehead with a trembling hand.*] Wonderful, that does it! Our one chance is privacy and you babble away to a man who'll think it his Christian duty to have us *confined* in—

[*She gasps and stumbles to the piano.*]

Clare!

[*She strikes a treble note repeatedly on the piano. He snatches her hand from the keyboard and slams the lid down.*]

CLARE: You shouldn't have spoken that word! "Confined"! That word is not in the—

FELICE: Oh. A prohibited word. When a word can't be used, when it's prohibited its silence increases its size. It gets larger and larger till it's so enormous that no house can hold it.

CLARE: Then say the word, over and over, you—*perverse monster,* you!

[FELICE *turns away.*]

Scared to? Afraid of a—?

FELICE: I won't do lunatic things. I have to try to pretend there's some sanity here.

CLARE: Oh, is that what you're trying? I thought you were trying to go as far off as possible without going past all limits.

[*He turns to face her, furiously. She smiles and forms the word "confined" with her lips; then she says it in a whisper. He snatches up a soft pillow.*]

Confined, confined!

[*He thrusts the pillow over her mouth, holding her by the shoulder. She struggles as if suffocating.*]

FELICE: All right? O.K., now? Enough?

[*She nods. He tosses the pillow away. They stare at each other silently for a moment. She has forgotten the next bit of business. He points to the piano. She turns and strikes a chord on it.*]

An interval of five minutes.

CLARE: *Fifteen!*

FELICE [*rushing into the wings to lower the curtain*]: Ten!

CURTAIN INTERVAL

During the interval, there has obviously been a physical struggle between the stars. She is still clutching an elbow and wincing with pain: a scratch is visible on his face. Both of them are panting.

FELICE [*in a whisper*]. Ready?

[*She nods: the performance is resumed.*]

A bowl of soap water and one spool are for blowing soap bubbles.

CLARE: Yesterday you said, "There's nothing to do, nothing at all to do."

FELICE: When we were children we blow soap bubbles on the back steps, not in the parlor.

CLARE: Can you imagine us sitting back there now, exposed to public view, blowing soap bubbles? We can't turn back to children in public view, but privately, in the parlor window . . .

FELICE: Soap bubbles floating out of the parlor window would not indicate to the world that we were in full possession of our senses.

[*She crosses to him and dabs his scratched cheek with a bit of cotton. His eyes shut as if this tender gesture were creating a sensuous sleepiness.*]

CLARE: Have you dried up, Felice?

[*He sways slightly.*]

I'm afraid I have, too.

FELICE: Improvise something till I—

CLARE: All right. Sit down. Breathe quietly. Rest a little, Felice, I'll—

[*He sits on the sofa and clasps the sides of his head.* CLARE *strikes a soft note on the piano, then leans against it, facing downstage.*]

—When Father gave up his psychic readings and astrological predictions, a few days before the *un-, in-explicable*—accident!—in the house—Well, he didn't give them up, exactly.

FELICE: No, not exactly by choice.

CLARE: Mother had locked up his quadrant and chart of night skies and his psychic paraphernalia.

FELICE: Except for this worn-out shirt of his I have on, which bears his sign of the zodiac on it and his rising sign and a chart of the sky as it was on the hour before daybreak of the day of his nativity here in New Bethesda!

CLARE: You know, he seemed to—accept. At least he said nothing. Not even when she spoke of State Haven to him. "Yes, I can see your mind is going again. Check yourself into State Haven for a long rest—voluntarily, or I'll—" He became very quiet. But restlessly quiet. He sat almost continually where you're sitting and stared at that threadbare rose in the carpet's center, and it seemed to smolder, yes, that rose seemed to smolder like his eyes and yours, and when a carpet catches fire in a wooden house, the house will catch fire, too. Felice, I swear that this is a house made of wood and that rose is smoldering, now!

[*She strikes a C-sharp on the piano. He glares at her furiously but she strikes the note again, louder.*]

FELICE [closing his eyes]: —Line?

CLARE: Didn't you tell me you'd thought of something we have to do today?

FELICE: —Yes, it's something we can't put off any longer.

34

CLARE: The letter of protest to the—

FELICE: No, no, letters of protest are barely even opened, no, what we *must* do today is go out of the house.

CLARE: To some particular place, or—

FELICE: To Grossman's Market.

CLARE: *There?*

FELICE: Yes, *there!*

CLARE: We tried that before and turned back.

FELICE: We didn't have a strong enough reason and it wasn't such a favorable afternoon.

CLARE: This afternoon is—?

FELICE: Much more favorable—And I simply know that it's necessary for us to go to Grossman's Market today since— I've kept this from you, but—sometimes the postman still comes through the barricade of sunflowers and that he did some days ago with a notification that no more—

CLARE: —Deliveries?

FELICE: Will be delivered to the steps of—

CLARE: I knew! Payment for costlies has been long—overdue.

FELICE: So out we do have to go to Grossman's Market, directly to Mr. Grossman's office and speak personally to him.

CLARE: His office! Where's his office? Probably tucked away in some never-discovered corner of that shadowy labyrinth of a—

FELICE: We'll ask a clerk to tell us, to take us, to Mr. Grossman's office.

35

CLARE: If the clerk saw us, he'd pretend that he didn't.

FELICE: Not if we enter with some air of assurance—We're going to enter Grossman's Market today like a pair of—

CLARE: Prosperous, paying customers?

FELICE: Yes, we'll say to the clerk, "Please show us the office of Mr. Grossman." We are going to tell him convincingly that in spite of all spite and, and—contrary—accusations—Father's insurance policy will be paid to us by the Acme Insurance Company on, say, the first of next month, yes, on September the first.

CLARE: But we know that it won't be!—Why, they wrote only three sentences to us in reply to the twelve-page appeal that we wrote and rewrote, for a week—

[*They have crossed downstage to opposite sides of the interior set, facing out.*]

CLARE [*at a fast pace*]: We've been informed by the—

FELICE [*at a fast pace*]: Acme Insurance Company—

CLARE [*at a fast pace*]:—that the insurance money is—

FELICE [*at a fast pace*]: Forfeited.

CLARE [*at a fast pace*]: Yes, the payment of the insurance policy is forfeited in the—

FELICE [*at a fast pace*]: Event—

CLARE [*at a fast pace*]: Yes, in the event of a man— [*She stops, pressing her fist to her mouth.*]

FELICE [*at a fast pace*]: In the event of a man killing his wife, then himself, and—

CLARE: Unkindly forgetting his children.

FELICE:—That's what's called a legal technicality . . .

[*They turn again to each other.*]

CLARE: What do you know about anything legal, Felice?

FELICE: I know there are situations in which legal technicalities have to be, to be—disregarded in the interests of human, human—We must say that what we saw, there was only us to see and what we saw was *Mother* with the revolver, first killing Father and then herself and—

CLARE: A simple lie is one thing, but the absolute opposite of the truth is another.

FELICE [*wildly*]: *What's the truth in pieces of metal exploding from the hand of a man driven mad by—! [There is a pause.]* Well? Well? Do we do it or forget it?

CLARE: Sometimes our fear is—

FELICE: Our private badge of—

CLARE: —Courage . . .

FELICE: Right!—The door is still open. Are we going out?

[*After a pause, she backs away from him a step.*]

CLARE: See if there are people on the street.

FELICE: Of course there are, there are always people on streets, that's what streets are made for, for people on them.

CLARE: I meant those boys. You know, those vicious boys that—

FELICE: Oh, yes. You stopped on the walk and shouted "Stop!" to the boys. Covered your ears with your hands and shouted: "Stop, stop!" They stopped, they crossed the street. I said: "For God's sake, what did you think they were doing? Why did you shout 'Stop!' at them?"

CLARE [*overlapping*]: They were staring and grinning at me and spelling out a—

FELICE [*overlapping*]: You said they were spelling out an obscene word at you.

CLARE [*overlapping*]: Yes, an obscene word, the same obscene word that somebody scrawled on our back fence.

FELICE [*overlapping*]: Yes, you told me that, too. I looked at the back fence and nothing was scrawled on it, Clare.

CLARE [*overlapping*]: If you heard nothing the last time we went out, why wouldn't you go on alone to the grocery store? Why did you run back with me to the house?

FELICE [*overlapping*]: You were panicky. I was scared what you might do.

CLARE [*overlapping*]: What did you think I might do?

FELICE [*overlapping*]: What Father and Mother did when—

CLARE [*overlapping*]: Stop here, we can't go on!

FELICE: Go on!

CLARE: Line!

FELICE: A few days ago you—

CLARE: No, you, you, not I! I can't sleep at night in a house where a revolver is hidden. Tell me where you hid it. We'll smash it, destroy it together—line!

FELICE [*calmly*]: I removed the cartridges from the revolver, and put them away, where I've deliberately forgotten and won't remember.

CLARE: "Deliberately forgotten!" Worthless! In a dream you'll remember. Felice, there's death in the house and you know where it's waiting.

FELICE [*wildly*]: *So!*—Do you prefer locked doors of separate buildings?

CLARE: You've been obsessed with locked doors since your stay at State Haven!

FELICE: Yes, I have the advantage of having experienced, once, the comforts, the security, the humanizing influence of—

CLARE: Locked doors!

FELICE: At State Haven!

CLARE: I'm sorry but you had allowed yourself to lose contact with all reality.

FELICE: What reality was there left in this—?

CLARE: Stopped speaking! Stared without recognition!

FELICE: Yes, being dumb-struck and blinded by—!

CLARE: Was *I? I* was here, too!

FELICE: Oh, I don't think you knew where you were any more! You—

CLARE: I knew enough to get out of bed in the morning instead of crouching under covers all day!

FELICE: Was that a sign of clearer—?

CLARE: It was a sign of ability to go on with—

FELICE: Customary habits!

CLARE: An appearance of—!

FELICE: *Fuck appearances!*

CLARE: *Hush!*—You've hidden the revolver, give it up. I'll take it down to the cellar and smash it with the wood-chopper, and then be able to sleep again in this house!

39

FELICE: —People don't know, sometimes, what keeps them awake . . .

[*He starts to lapse. The pace slows from exhaustion and they retreat from their opposite sides of the downstage interior.*]

CLARE: The need to search for—

FELICE: The contents of empty pockets?

CLARE: Not always empty! Sometimes there's a birthstone in them that isn't lucky!

[*There is a pause: they stare, panting, at each other. Very slowly, with lost eyes, he closes the door—nearly.*]

FELICE: —You have the face of an angel—I could no more ever, no matter how much you begged, me, fire a revolver at you than any impossible, unimaginable thing. Not even to lead you outside a door that can't be closed completely without its locking itself till the end of—I haven't completely closed it.—Clare, the door's still open.

CLARE [*with a slight, sad smile*]: Yes, a little, enough to admit the talk of—

FELICE [*overlap*]: Are we going out, now, or giving up all but one possible thing?

CLARE: —We're—going out, now. There never really was any question about it, you know.

FELICE: Good. At last you admit it.

[*There is a pause.*]

CLARE [*assuming a different air*]: But you're not properly dressed. For this auspicious occasion I want you to look your best. Close the door a moment.

40

FELICE: If it were closed, it might never open again.

CLARE: I'm just—just going upstairs to fetch your fair-weather jacket and a tie to go with it. [*She turns upstage.*] Oh, but no stairs on the set!

FELICE: The set's incomplete.

CLARE: I know, I know, you told me. [*She faces upstage.*] I have gone upstairs and you are alone in the parlor.

FELICE: Yes, I am alone in the parlor with the front door open.—I hear voices from the street, the calls and laughter of demons. "Loonies, loonies, loonies, *loooo-nies!*"—I—shut the door, remembering what I'd said.

CLARE: You said that it might never be opened again. [*She turns abruptly downstage.*] Oh, there you *are!*

FELICE: Yes. Of course. *Waiting* for you.

CLARE: I wasn't long, was I?

FELICE: —No, but I wondered if you would actually come back down.

CLARE: Here I am, and here is your jacket and here is your tie. [*She holds out empty hands.*]

FELICE: The articles are invisible.

CLARE [*with a mocking smile*]: Put on your invisible jacket and your invisible tie.

FELICE: —I go through the motions of—

CLARE: Ah, now, what a difference! Run a comb through your hair!

FELICE: —Where is—?

CLARE: The inside jacket pocket. I put it there.

41

FELICE: —Oh?—Yes.—Thanks . . . [*He makes the gesture of removing a comb from his invisible jacket.*]

CLARE: Oh, let *me* do it! [*She arranges his hair with her fingers.*]

FELICE: That's enough. That will do.

CLARE: Hold still just one moment longer.

FELICE: No, no, that's enough, Clare.

CLARE: Yes, well, now you look like a gentleman with excellent credit at every store in the town of New Bethesda!

FELICE: Hmmm . . .

CLARE: The door is shut.—Why did you shut the door?

FELICE: —The wind was blowing dust in.

CLARE: There is no wind at all.

FELICE: There *was,* so I—

CLARE: Shut the door. Will you be able to open it again?

FELICE: Yes. Of course. [*He starts the tape recorder again. Then, after a hesitant moment, he draws the door open.*]

CLARE: —What are you waiting for?

FELICE: For you to go out.

CLARE: You go first. I'll follow.

FELICE: —How do I know you would?

CLARE: When a thing has been settled, I don't back out.

FELICE: That may be, but you are going out first.

CLARE: Will you come out right behind me or will you bolt the door on me and—

[*He seizes her hand and draws her forcibly to the door. She gasps.*]

FELICE: Out!

CLARE: See if—!

FELICE: There are no boys on the street!

CLARE: May I set my hat straight please?

FELICE: Stop this foolishness. Afternoons aren't everlasting, you know.—OUT!

[*He thrusts her through the open door. She cries out softly. He comes out, shutting the door and faces the audience.*]

Now there is, there must be, a slight pause in the performance while I slip offstage to light the front of the house. [*He starts offstage.*]

CLARE [*terrified whisper*]: Oh, God, don't leave me alone here!

FELICE: For a moment, one moment. [*He goes into the wings. An amber light is turned on the area around the door. He returns to her side, takes her hand and leads her forward a little.*] It's a nice afternoon.

CLARE [*tensely*]: Yes!

FELICE: You couldn't ask for a nicer afternoon, if afternoons could be asked for.

CLARE: No!

FELICE: I don't know what we're waiting here for. Do you?

[CLARE *shakes her head and tries to laugh.*]

We're waiting here like it was a car stop. But it's only a block and a half to Grossman's Market.

43

CLARE: I don't know why, but I'm shaking, I can't control it. It would make a bad impression on Mr. Grossman.

FELICE: You're not going to back out now. I won't allow you.

CLARE: Felice, while you're gone, I could, could, could—make a phone call to "Citizens' Relief," you know, those people we wouldn't let in the house. I could tell them to come right over, and answer all their questions, and we would receive their relief even if Mr. Grossman doesn't believe the story.

FELICE: Clare, quit stalling. Let's go now.

CLARE: —I left something in the house.

FELICE: What?

CLARE: I left my—my—

FELICE: You see, you don't know what you left, so it can't be important.

CLARE: Oh, it is, it's very—it's, it's the—cotton I put in my nose when I have a nosebleed, and I feel like I might have one almost any minute. *The lime dust!*

[*She turns quickly to the door, but he blocks her, stretching his arms across the doorway. She utters a soft cry and runs around to the window. He reaches the window before she can climb in.*]

FELICE: You're not going to climb in that window!

CLARE: I am! Let me, I have to! I have a pain in my heart!

FELICE: Don't make me drag you by force to Grossman's Market!

CLARE: The moment I get back in I'll call the people from "Citizens' Relief"!—I *promise!*

44

FELICE: *Liar! Liar, and coward*

CLARE: Oh, Felice, I—

[*She runs back to the door. He remains by the window. She enters the interior set and stares out at him, hands clasped tightly together. He steps over the low windowsill and they face each other silently for a moment.*]

FELICE: If we're not able to walk one block and a half to Grossman's Market, we're not able to live in this house or anywhere else but in two separate buildings. So now listen to me, Clare. Either you come back out and go through the program at Grossman's or I will leave here and never come back here again and you'll stay on here alone.

CLARE: You know what I'd do if I was left here alone.

FELICE: Yes, I know what she'd do, so I seize her arm and shout into her face: "Out again, the front door!" I try to drag her to it.

CLARE: I catch hold of something, cling to it! Cling to it for dear life!

FELICE: Cling to it!

CLARE: It's not on the set, the newel post of the stairs. I wrap both arms about it and he can't tear me loose.

FELICE: Stay here, stay here alone When I go out of this house I'll never come back. I'll walk and walk, I'll go and go! Away, away, away!

CLARE: I'll wait!

FELICE: For *what?*

CLARE: For *you!*

45

FELICE: That will be a long wait, a longer wait than you imagine. I'm leaving you now. *Good-bye!* [*He steps out over the low sill of the window.*]

CLARE [*calling out after him*]: Don't stay long! Hurry back!

FELICE: Hah! [*He comes forward and speaks pantingly to the audience.*] The audience is supposed to imagine that the front of the house, where I am standing now, is shielded by sunflowers, too, but that was impractical as it would cut off the view. I stand here—move not a step further. Impossible without her. No, I can't leave her alone. I feel so exposed, so cold. And behind me I feel the house. It seems to be breathing a faint, warm breath on my back. I feel it the way you feel a loved person standing close behind you. Yes, I'm already defeated. The house is so old, so faded, so warm that, yes, it seems to be breathing. It seems to be whispering to me: "You can't go away. Give up. Come in and stay." Such a *gentle* command! What do I do? Naturally I obey. [*He turns and enters by the door.*] I come back into the house, very quietly. I don't look at my sister.

CLARE: We're ashamed to look at each other. We're ashamed of having retreated—surrendered so quickly.

FELICE: There is a pause, a silence, our eyes avoiding each other's.

CLARE: Guiltily.

FELICE: No rock hits the house. No insults and obscenities are shouted.

CLARE: The afternoon light.

FELICE: Yes, the afternoon light is unbelievably golden on the—

CLARE: The furniture which is so much older than we are—

FELICE: I realize, now, that the house has turned to a prison.

CLARE: I know it's a prison, too, but it's one that isn't strange to us.—Felice, what did I do with that card from "Citizens' Relief"?

FELICE: I think you put it under—

CLARE: Oh. Grandmother's wedding picture. [*She takes the card and goes to the phone.*]—I'm going to call them!

FELICE: —I suppose it's time to.

[*She lifts the phone hesitantly.*]

CLARE: I lift the receiver and it makes no sound. I feel like screaming into the phone: "Help, help!"

FELICE: —Is it—?

CLARE [*hanging up the receiver*]: Sometimes a phone will go dead temporarily, just for a little while, and come back to life, you know.

FELICE: Yes, I know. Of course.

CLARE: —So we stay here and wait till it's connected again?

FELICE: We might have to wait till after the Relief Office closes. It might be a better idea to ask the people next door if we can use their phone since something's gone wrong with ours.

CLARE: That's right. Why don't you do that?

FELICE: *You* do that. It's the sort of thing you could do better. Look! [*He points at the window.*] The woman next

47

door is taking some clothes off her wash line. Call her through the window.

[CLARE *catches her breath. Then she rushes to the window and calls out in a stifled voice.*]

CLARE: Please, may I, please, may we—!

FELICE: Not loud enough, call louder.

CLARE [*turning from the window*]:—Did you really imagine that I could call and beg for "Citizens' Relief" in front of those malicious people next door, on their phone, in their presence? Why, they gave their son a slingshot to stone the house!

[*There is a slight pause.*]

FELICE: You asked me what people did when they had nothing at all left to do.

CLARE: I asked you no such thing. [*After a moment, she dips a spool in the soapy water.*]

FELICE: Instead of calling the woman next door through the parlor window, you blow a soap bubble through it. It's lovely as your birthstone.—But it's a sign of surrender, and we know it.—And now I touch her hand lightly, which is a signal that I am about to speak a new line in *The Two-Character Play.* [*He touches her hand.*] Clare, didn't you tell me that yesterday or last night or today you came across a box of cartridges for Father's revolver?

CLARE: No! No, I—

FELICE: Clare, you say "yes," not "no." And then I pick up the property of the play which she's always hated and dreaded, so much that she refuses to remember that it exists in the play.

48

CLARE: I've said it's—*unnecessary!*

[FELICE *has picked up a revolver from under the sheet music on the piano top.*]

Has it always been there?

FELICE: The revolver and the box of cartridges that you found last night have never been anywhere else, not in any performance of the play. Now I remove the blank cartridges and insert the real ones as calmly as if I were removing dead flowers from a vase and putting in fresh ones. Yes, as calmly as—

[*But his fingers are shaking so that the revolver falls to the floor.* CLARE *gasps, then laughs breathlessly.*]

Stop it!

[CLARE *covers her mouth with her hand.*]

Now I—[*He pauses.*]

CLARE: Have you forgotten what you do next? Too bad. I don't remember.

FELICE: I haven't forgotten what I do next. I put the revolver in the center of the little table across which we had discussed the attitude of nature toward its creatures that are regarded as *unnatural* creatures, and then I—[*After placing the revolver on the table, he pauses.*]

CLARE: What do you do next? Do you remember?

FELICE: Yes, I—[*He starts the tape recorder.*]—I pick up my spool and dip it in the water and blow a soap bubble out the parlor window without the slightest concern about what neighbors may think. Of course, sometimes the soap bubble bursts before it rises, but this time please imagine you see it rising through gold light, above the gold sunflower heads.

49

Now I turn to my sister who has the face of an angel and say to her: "Look! Do you see?"

CLARE: Yes, I do, it's lovely and it still hasn't broken.

FELICE: Sometimes we do still see the same things at the same time.

CLARE: Yes, and we would till locked in separate buildings and marched out at different hours, you by bullet-eyed guards and me by bullet-eyed matrons. [*She strikes a note on the piano.*] Oh, what a long, long way we've traveled together, too long, now, for separation. Yes, all the way back to sunflowers and soap bubbles, and there's no turning back on the road even if the road's backward, and—[CLARE *looks out at the audience.*]—The favorites of nature have gone away.

[FELICE *does not respond.*]

Felice, the performance is *over*. [*She stops the taped guitar.*]

[*After the performance.*]

CLARE [*continued*]: Put on your coat. I'm going to put on mine.

[*He stares at her, stupefied.*]

Felice, come out of the play. The audience has left, the house is completely empty.

FELICE:—Walked? Out? All?

CLARE [*she has picked up their coats from behind the sofa*]: You honestly didn't notice them get up and go?

FELICE: I was lost in the play.

CLARE: You were but they weren't, so they left.

FELICE: You made cuts in the play that destroyed the texture.

CLARE: I cut when the house sounded like a t.b. ward.

FELICE: If you'd been concentrating you would have held them.

CLARE: Christ, did I try! Till the seats banged up and—

FELICE: —I hear no sound from the house when I'm lost in a play.

CLARE: Then *don't* get lost in a play! Get lost in *woods,* among *wolves!*

FELICE: HA!

CLARE: Oh, let's stop this silly bitching, taking our rage at those idiots out on each other, it's pointless. Here, here, put this on you!

[*She has jerked a torn, discolored white silk scarf from his sleeve, and tries to stuff it under his mangy fur collar.*]

FELICE: Stop that! Don't put things on me I can put on myself if I want them on me! This scarf goes into the wardrobe for *The Lower Depths . . .*

[*He throws it to the floor. She picks it up and now he permits her to place the dirty scarf beneath his collar; he is still panting and staring desolately out.*]

CLARE [*she opens her cigarette case*]: Only three smokables left.—*Gentle man,* be seated.

[*She gestures toward the sofa upstage and they move unsteadily toward it. She stumbles; he clutches her shoulders; they sit down. She offers him a cigarette; he takes it.*]

—Lucifers?

[*Mechanically he removes a scant book of matches from his coat pocket, strikes one and holds it before him: for a*

51

couple of moments both of them seem unconscious of it; then she slowly turns her look on it.]

—Did you strike it to light our cigarettes, dear, or just to relieve the gloom of the atmosphere?

FELICE [*lighting her cigarette*]: Sorry...[*He starts to light his own cigarette, the match burns his fingers.*] Mmmmmmmm!

[*She blows the match out and lights his cigarette with hers; they smoke together quietly for a moment.*]

CLARE: The first time I turned downstage I simply couldn't help seeing those—

FELICE: Clare, let it go, they're gone.

CLARE: —fur-bearing mammals out there, went into panic, didn't come out till this moment. Ahhh . . .

FELICE: Hmmm . . .

CLARE: Now call Fox. See if there's money enough to get us out of this place.

[*There is a pause.* FELICE *is afraid to call Fox, suspecting he's long gone.*]

Well, for God's sake, call him!

FELICE [*calling into the house*]: Fox!—*Fox!*

CLARE: Perhaps the audience caught him and fed him to their dog teams—*Fox, Fox, Fox!*

TOGETHER: *Fox!*

[*There is an echo from their call; they listen, with diminishing hope, for a response. Finally:*]

CLARE: I feel like falling into bed at the nearest hotel and sleeping the next thousand years.

FELICE: Well, go get your things.

CLARE: Get what things?

FELICE: Your purse, your handbag, for instance.

CLARE: I don't have one to get.

FELICE: You've lost it again?

CLARE: This still seems like a performance of *The Two-Character Play*. The worst thing that's disappeared in our lives is not the Company, not Fox, not brandy in your flask, not successes that give confidence to go on—no, none of that. The worst thing that's disappeared in our lives is being aware of what's going *on* in our lives. We don't dare talk about it, it's like a secret that we're conspiring to keep from each other, even though each of us knows that the other one knows it. [*She strikes a piano key. There is a pause.*] Felice, is it possible that *The Two-Character Play* doesn't have an ending?

FELICE: Even if we were what the Company called us in the cable, we'd never perform a play that had no end to it, Clare.

CLARE: It never seems to end but just to stop, and it always seems to stop just short of something important when you suddenly say: "The preformance is over."

FELICE: It's possible for a play to have no ending in the usual sense of an ending, in order to make a point about nothing really ending.

CLARE: I didn't know you believed in the everlasting.

FELICE: That's not what I meant at all.

CLARE: I don't think you know *what* you meant. Things do end, they do actually have to.

FELICE [*rising*]: Up! Hotel! Grand entrance! We'll face everything tomorrow.

CLARE: Everything will face *us* tomorrow and not with a pretty face. No, Sir. And as for right now, we don't have fares for a dog sled to the hotel, and just before the performance you told me that Fox hasn't made us hotel reservations here, wherever here is!

FELICE: I think I remember seeing a hotel across the plaza from the theatre when we came from the station. We'll go there, we'll enter in such grand style that we'll need no reservations. Wait here while I—[*He rushes into the wings.*]

CLARE: *Where are you—?*

[*She follows him as far as the giant's statue, and stops there. The cold, stone vault of the building is no longer silent. We hear running footsteps, the hollow, unintelligible echo of shouitng, metal clanging, etc. Clasping the pedestal of the statue,* CLARE *faces downstage, moving spasmodically at each ominous sound, sometimes catching her breath sharply. The sounds stop: there is total silence. She starts toward the door far upstage, then retreats to the statue.*]

Giant, he'll come back, won't he? You don't look sure about that. It's so terribly quiet after all those noises.—*Felice!*

FELICE'S VOICE [*distant*]:Yes!

CLARE: Hurry back! I'm alone here!—turning to a frozen supplicant at the feet of a merciless—poor Felice. He lost his argument about the impossible being necessary tonight. The impossible and the necessary pass each other without recognition on streets, and as for *The Two-Character Play*, when he read it aloud I said to myself, "This is his last one, there's nothing more after this."—Well, there are festivals to remember. Riding a fiacre, you driving the horses, drunk across

54

Rilke's Bridge of Angels over the Tiber, a crack of thunder and suddenly a sleet storm, pelting our laughing faces with tiny marbles of ice. *Un mezzo litro. Una bottiglia. Une bouteille de. Frutta di mare. Comme c'est beau ici! Como bello! Maraviglioso!*—"Your sister and you are insane."—How ridiculous! Clinging for protection to the pedestal of a monster . . .

[*There is the sound of footsteps.*]

He's coming back, thank God!

[FELICE *returns, as if blind, to the stage.*]

What luck, Felice?

[*He crosses past her as if he didn't see her, enters the interior set, and sinks, panting, onto the sofa. She follows him slowly, drawing her coat close about her.*]

Well? Another disaster?

FELICE [*without facing her*]: Clare, I'm afraid we may have to stay here a while.

CLARE: In this frozen country?

FELICE: I meant here in the theatre.

CLARE: Oh?

FELICE: Yes, you see, the stage door and the front doors are all locked from outside, there isn't a window in the building, and the backstage phone is lifeless as the phone in *The Two-Character Play* was, finally was.

CLARE: Do you notice any change in the lighting?

FELICE: Yes, the lights have dimmed.

CLARE: They're still dimming.

FELICE: And I haven't touched the light switch.

55

CLARE [*shouting*]: *Out, out, out! Human outcry!*

FELICE: It's no good screaming, *cara.*

CLARE: I wasn't screaming, I was shouting!

FELICE: The firing of a revolver in this building wouldn't be heard outside it.

CLARE: Does this mean we'll have to stay here freezing till they open up the building in the morning?

FELICE: Clare, there's no assurance they'll open up the building in the morning or even in the evening or any morning or evening after that.

CLARE [*with an abrupt flash of hope*]:—Oh, Felice, the hole in the backstage wall . . . [*She points upstage.*]

FELICE: Sometimes the same idea still occurs to us both. [*He looks at her with a "dark" smile. He is breathing heavily from his exertion.*] I tried to increase the width of that— crevice, it's narrow as those vents in old castle walls that— arrows were shot through at—besiegers, and all I accomplished for my labors was *this* . . . [*He lifts the bloodied palms of his hands.*]

CLARE [*cutting in*]: Are you working on some neo-Elizabethan historical drama, Felice? If you are, write me out of the cast and, and—wipe your bloody hands on something clean.—Stop grinning at me like that!

FELICE: It's not you I'm grinning at, Clare.

CLARE: You're looking at me with a savage grin!—Do you *hate* me, Felice?

FELICE: Of *course* I do, if I *love* you, and I think that I do. [*He moves a little downstage: his next line should be underplayed.*]—"A garden enclosed is my sister . . ."

56

[*There is a pause.*]

I think fear *is* limited, don't you, Clare?

CLARE: —Yes. I do.

FELICE: Isn't it limited to the ability of a person to care any more?

CLARE: —For anything but—[*She means for "one other person"; but that touch of sentiment, is better left spoken by just a glance between them*] —So it's a prison, this last theatre of ours?

FELICE: It would seem to be one.

CLARE [*objectively, now*]: I've always suspected that theatres are prisons for players . . .

FELICE: Finally, yes. And for writers of plays . . .

[*She moves downstage.*]

CLARE: So finally we are—the prohibited word . . .

[*He strikes a note on the piano. They are almost smiling, wryly: there is no self-pity.*]

And, oh, God, the air isn't cold like ordinary cold but like the sort of cold there must be at the far, the farthest, the go-no-more last edge of space!

FELICE: Clare, you're not frightened, are you?

CLARE: No, I'm too tired to be frightened, at least I'm not yet frightened.

FELICE [*placing the revolver under the sheet music at the piano*]: Then you will *never* be frightened.

CLARE: It's strange, you know, since I've always had such a dread of—prohibited word!—it's the greatest dread of my life.

FELICE: And of mine, too.

CLARE: But, no, right now what I feel is—[*She crosses to the sofa and sinks exhaustedly onto it.*]—is simply bone-tired and bone-cold.

[*Her rigid hands tremble in her lap. He sits beside her and takes hold of one of her hands and rubs it.*]

—Otherwise I'd get up and see for myself if these mysteries that you've reported to me are exactly as you've reported, or—

FELICE: Do you think I've imagined them, dreamed them, Clare?

CLARE: —Sometimes you work on a play by inventing situations in life that, that—correspond to those in the play, and you're so skillfull at it that even I'm taken in . . . [*She withdraws one hand and offers him the other.*] Circulation has stopped in this hand, too.

[*He rubs her other hand, looking into her eyes as if presenting her with a challenge: She doesn't return the look.*]

—About our cholera shots, they may not be so tolerant on the way back . . . And with my passport missing . . .

FELICE: Your mind's wandering, Clare.

CLARE: —Going back . . .

FELICE: Going back's reversing a law of—

CLARE: Nature?

FELICE: About that likely, Clare.

[*There are clanking noises.*]

CLARE: —What's—?

FELICE: Pipes expanding with—

58

CLARE: Metal contracts with—

FELICE [*Gently*]: Clare, your mind's going out.

CLARE: That shows it's—wiser than God . . .

FELICE: —When there's a thing to be done—

CLARE: There's nothing to be done.

FELICE: There's always something to be done. There's no such thing as an inescapable corner with two people in it. What's necessary is to know that there is a thing to be done, and then not think about it, just know it has to be done and—

CLARE: You have a dark thought in your head and I think I know what it is.

FELICE: Sometimes we still have the same thought at the same time, and that could be an advantage to us now.

CLARE [*drawing her cloak about her*]: Will it get any colder?

FELICE: It's not going to get any warmer.—You know, during the performance, even under hot lights, the stage was cold, but I was so lost in the play that it seemed warm as a summer afternoon in . . .

[*During this speech he has crossed to the tape recorder and turned it back on at a low level. The selection could be Villa-Lobos'* Brasilianas *and should continue through the curtain.*]

CLARE: —You are suggesting that we—?

FELICE: Go back into the play.

CLARE: But with the stage so dim—

FELICE: If we can imagine summer, we can imagine more light.

59

CLARE: If we're lost in the play?

FELICE: Yes, completely—in *The Two-Character Play.*

[*She nods and struggles to rise from the sofa but topples back down. He draws her up.*]

CLARE: *Back into the play,* try it, give it a Sunday try!

FELICE: Other alternatives—

CLARE: Lacking!—Can we keep on our coats?

FELICE: We could but I think the feeling of summer would come more easily to us if we took our coats off.

CLARE: *Off coats! Put the cablegram back on the sofa!*

[*They remove their coats and fling them over the sofa. He places the cablegram against the back of it.*]

Do we stop where we stopped tonight or do we look for an ending?

FELICE: I think that you will find it wherever you hid it, Clare.

CLARE: Wherever *you* hid it, not me. [*She looks at him and gasps, lifting a hand toward her mouth.*]

FELICE: Is something wrong?

CLARE: No!—no . . .

[*He smiles at her, then removes the revolver from under the sheet music on the piano.*]

—Was it *always* there?

FELICE: Yes, in every performance. Where would you like me to place it?

CLARE: Under a sofa pillow? By the Company's cable?

60

FELICE: Yes, but remember which one and snatch it up quickly, quickly, and—[*He thrusts the revolver under a pillow.*]

CLARE [*Her smile glacial, now*]: Hit hard and get out fast?

FELICE: Yes, that's the cry!

CLARE: Do we start at the top of the play?

FELICE: With your phone bit, yes. *The performance commences!*

CLARE: When a performance works out inevitably, it works out well. [*She lifts the telephone.*]

FELICE: Who are you calling, Clare?

CLARE [*very fast*]: Not a soul still existing in the world gone away.

FELICE [*very fast*]: Then why did you pick up the phone?

CLARE [*very fast*]: To see if it's still connected.

FELICE [*very fast*]: We would have been notified if—

CLARE [*very fast*]: It's a mistake to depend on—notification. Especially when a house looks vacant at night. [*She hangs up the phone.*]

FELICE [*very fast*]: Night, what a restless night.

CLARE [*very fast*]: Wasn't it, though?

FELICE [*very fast*]: I didn't sleep at all well and neither did you. I heard you wandering about the house as if you were looking for something.

CLARE [*very fast*]: Yes, I was and I found it. [*She pauses.*] Are you lost in the play?

FELICE: Yes, it's a warm August day.

61

CLARE [*raising a hand, tenderly, to his head*]: Felice, your hair's grown so long, you really must find the time somehow to.—We mustn't neglect appearances even if we rarely go out of the house. We won't stay in so much now. I'm sure they'll believe that Mother shot Father and then herself, that we saw it happen. We can believe it ourselves, and then the insurance company will come through with the policy payment, and livables, commendables, and necessities of persistence will be delivered through the barricade of—

FELICE: Go straight to the tall sunflowers.

CLARE: Quick as that?

FELICE: That quick!

CLARE: Felice, look out of the window! There's a giant sunflower out there that's grown as tall as the house!

[FELICE *crosses quickly to the window and looks out.*]

FELICE: *Oh, yes, I see it. Its color's so brilliant that it seems to be shouting!*

CLARE: *Keep your eyes on it a minute, it's a sight to be seen!*

[*She quickly retrieves the revolver from beneath the sofa cushion, and resolutely aims it at* FELICE, *holding the revolver at arm's length. There is a pause.*]

FELICE [*harshly*]: *Do it while you still can!*

CLARE [*crying out*]: *I can't!*

[*She turns convulsively away from him, dropping the revolver as if it had scorched her hand. As it crashes to the floor,* FELICE *turns from the window, his motion as convulsive as hers. Their figures are now almost entirely lost in dark but light touches their faces.*]

62

Can you?

[*He moves a few steps toward the revolver, then picks it
up and slowly, with effort points it at* CLARE. FELICE *tries
very hard to pull the trigger: he cannot. Slowly he lowers
his arm, and drops the revolver to the floor. There is a
pause.* FELICE *raises his eyes to watch the light fade from
the face of his sister as it is fading from his: in both their
faces is a tender admission of defeat. They reach out their
hands to one another, and the light lingers a moment on
their hands lifting toward each other. As they slowly em-
brace, there is total dark in which:*]

THE CURTAIN FALLS

New Directions Paperbooks—A Partial Listing

For complete listing request free catalog from
New Directions, 80 Eighth Avenue, New York 10011

†Bilingual

Frédéric Mistral, *The Memoirs*. NDP632.
Eugenio Montale, *It Depends.*† NDP507.
  Selected Poems.† NDP193.
Paul Morand, *Fancy Goods / Open All Night.*
  NDP567.
Vladimir Nabokov, *Nikolai Gogol.* NDP78.
  Laughter in the Dark. NDP729.
  The Real Life of Sebastian Knight. NDP432.
P. Neruda, *The Captain's Verses.*† NDP345.
  Residence on Earth.† NDP340.
New Directions in Prose & Poetry (Anthology).
  Available from #17 forward to #55.
Robert Nichols, *Arrival.* NDP437.
  Exile. NDP485.
J. F. Nims, *The Six-Cornered Snowflake.* NDP700.
Charles Olson, *Selected Writings.* NDP231.
Toby Olson, *The Life of Jesus.* NDP417.
  Seaview. NDP532.
George Oppen, *Collected Poems.* NDP418.
István Örkeny, *The Flower Show /*
  The Toth Family. NDP536.
Wilfred Owen, *Collected Poems.* NDP210.
José Emilio Pacheco, *Battles in the Desert.* NDP637.
  Selected Poems.† NDP638.
Nicanor Parra, *Antipoems: New & Selected.* NDP603.
Boris Pasternak, *Safe Conduct.* NDP77.
Kenneth Patchen, *Aflame and Afun.* NDP292.
  Because It Is. NDP83.
  Collected Poems. NDP284.
  Hallelujah Anyway. NDP219.
  Selected Poems. NDP160.
Ota Pavel, *How I Came to Know Fish.* NDP713.
Octavio Paz, *Collected Poems.* NDP719.
  Configurations.† NDP303.
  A Draft of Shadows.† NDP489.
  Selected Poems. NDP574.
  Sunstone.† NDP735.
  A Tree Within.† NDP661.
St. John Perse, *Selected Poems.*† NDP545.
J. A. Porter, *Eelgrass.* NDP438.
Ezra Pound, *ABC of Reading.* NDP89.
  Confucius. NDP285.
  Confucius to Cummings. (Anth.) NDP126.
  A Draft of XXX Cantos. NDP690.
  Elektra. NDP683.
  Guide to Kulchur. NDP257.
  Literary Essays. NDP250.
  Personae. NDP697.
  Selected Cantos. NDP304.
  Selected Poems. NDP66.
  The Spirit of Romance. NDP266.
  Translations.† (Enlarged Edition) NDP145.
Raymond Queneau, *The Blue Flowers.* NDP595.
  Exercises in Style. NDP513.
Mary de Rachewiltz, *Ezra Pound.* NDP405.
Raja Rao, *Kanthapura.* NDP224.
Herbert Read, *The Green Child.* NDP208.
P. Reverdy, *Selected Poems.*† NDP346.
Kenneth Rexroth, *An Autobiographical Novel.* NDP725.
  Classics Revisited. NDP621.
  More Classics Revisited. NDP668.
  Flower Wreath Hill. NDP724.
  100 Poems from the Chinese. NDP192.
  100 Poems from the Japanese.† NDP147.
  Selected Poems. NDP581.
  Women Poets of China. NDP528.
  Women Poets of Japan. NDP527.
Rainer Maria Rilke, *Poems from*
  The Book of Hours. NDP408.
  Possibility of Being. (Poems). NDP436.
  Where Silence Reigns. (Prose). NDP464.
Arthur Rimbaud, *Illuminations.*† NDP56.
  Season in Hell & Drunken Boat.† NDP97.
Edouard Roditi, *Delights of Turkey.* NDP445.
Jerome Rothenberg, *Khurbn.* NDP679.
  New Selected Poems. NDP625.
Nayantara Sahgal, *Rich Like Us.* NDP665.
Saigyo, *Mirror for the Moon.*† NDP465.

Ihara Saikaku, *The Life of an Amorous*
  Woman. NDP270.
St. John of the Cross, *Poems.*† NDP341.
W. Saroyan, *Madness in the Family.* NDP691.
Jean-Paul Sartre, *Nausea.* NDP82.
  The Wall (Intimacy). NDP272.
P. D. Scott, *Coming to Jakarta.* NDP672.
Delmore Schwartz, *Selected Poems.* NDP241.
  Last & Lost Poems. NDP673.
  In Dreams Begin Responsibilities. NDP454.
Shattan, *Manimekhalaï.* NDP674.
K. Shiraishi, *Seasons of Sacred Lust.* NDP453.
Stevie Smith, *Collected Poems.* NDP562.
  New Selected Poems. NDP659.
Gary Snyder, *The Back Country.* NDP249.
  The Real Work. NDP499.
  Regarding Wave. NDP306.
  Turtle Island. NDP381.
Enid Starkie, *Rimbaud.* NDP254.
Stendhal. *Three Italian Chronicles.* NDP704.
Antonio Tabucchi, *Indian Nocturne.* NDP666.
Nathaniel Tarn, *Lyrics . . . Bride of God.* NDP391.
Dylan Thomas, *Adventures in the Skin Trade.*
  NDP183.
  A Child's Christmas in Wales. NDP181.
  Collected Poems 1934-1952. NDP316.
  Collected Stories. NDP626.
  Portrait of the Artist as a Young Dog. NDP51.
  Quite Early One Morning. NDP90.
  Under Milk Wood. NDP73.
Tian Wen: A Chinese Book of Origins. NDP624.
Uwe Timm, *The Snake Tree.* NDP686.
Lionel Trilling, *E. M. Forster.* NDP189.
Tu Fu, *Selected Poems.* NDP675.
N. Tucci, *The Rain Came Last.* NDP688.
Martin Turnell, *Baudelaire.* NDP336.
Paul Valéry, *Selected Writings.*† NDP184.
Elio Vittorini, *A Vittorini Omnibus.* NDP366.
Rosmarie Waldrop, *The Reproduction of Profiles.*
  NDP649.
Robert Penn Warren, *At Heaven's Gate.* NDP588.
Vernon Watkins, *Selected Poems.* NDP221.
Eliot Weinberger, *Works on Paper.* NDP627.
Nathanael West, *Miss Lonelyhearts &*
  Day of the Locust. NDP125.
J. Wheelwright, *Collected Poems.* NDP544.
Tennessee Williams, *Baby Doll.* NDP714.
  Camino Real. NDP301.
  Cat on a Hot Tin Roof. NDP398.
  Clothes for a Summer Hotel. NDP556.
  The Glass Menagerie. NDP218.
  Hard Candy. NDP225.
  In the Winter of Cities. NDP154.
  A Lovely Sunday for Creve Coeur. NDP497.
  One Arm & Other Stories. NDP237.
  Red Devil Battery Sign. NDP650.
  A Streetcar Named Desire. NDP501.
  Sweet Bird of Youth. NDP409.
  Twenty-Seven Wagons Full of Cotton. NDP217.
  Vieux Carre. NDP482.
William Carlos Williams,
  The Autobiography. NDP223.
  The Buildup. NDP259.
  Collected Poems: Vol. I. NDP730.
  Collected Poems: Vol. II. NDP731.
  The Doctor Stories. NDP585.
  Imaginations. NDP329.
  In the American Grain. NDP53.
  In the Money. NDP240.
  Paterson. Complete. NDP152.
  Pictures from Brueghel. NDP118.
  Selected Poems (new ed.). NDP602.
  White Mule. NDP226.
Wisdom Books: *Early Buddhists.* NDP444;
  Spanish Mystics. NDP442; *St. Francis.* NDP477;
  Taoists. NDP509; *Wisdom of the Desert.* NDP295;
  Zen Masters. NDP415.

For complete listing request free catalog from
New Directions, 80 Eighth Avenue, New York 10011

†Bilingual